Dog Diaries

Secret Writings of the WOOF Society

Betsy Byars
Betsy Duffey
Laurie Myers

Illustrated by Erik Brooks

SQUARE
FISH

Henry Holt and Company
New York

SQUARE
FISH

An Imprint of Macmillan
175 Fifth Avenue
New York, NY 10010
mackids.com

Library of Congress Cataloging-in-Publication Data
Byars, Betsy Cromer.
Dog diaries : secret writings of the WOOF Society / Betsy Byars; Betsy Duffey;
Laurie Myers; illustrated by Erik Brooks.
p.   cm.
Summary: At the first annual meeting of WOOF—Words of Our Friends—
assorted dogs preserve their heritage by sharing tales of canines throughout history,
including Abu, who ruled all of Egypt except for one pesky cat.
ISBN 978-1-250-07329-7 (paperback)   ISBN 978-1-4668-8961-3 (ebook)
[1. Dogs—Fiction. 2. Storytelling—Fiction.] I. Duffey, Betsy.
II. Myers, Laurie. III. Brooks, Erik, ill. IV. Title.
PZ7.B9836Dog 2007   [Fic]—dc22   2006011634

Originally published in the United States by Henry Holt and Company, LLC
First Square Fish Edition: 2016
Book designed by Patrick Collins
Square Fish logo designed by Filomena Tuosto

1 3 5 7 9 10 8 6 4 2

AR: 1.0 / LEXILE: 610L

In memory of Ace
—*B. B., B. D., L. M.*

For W. A. Weber
—*E. B.*

Contents

Dog Diaries

CHAPTER 1

Beauregard Presides

In a dark abandoned building, under a rickety staircase, was an entrance, more like a crack between two boards. Light shone behind the boards, beckoning to those outside. Through this mysterious entrance came dogs—large Dobermans, small Pekingese, Scotties, and Pugs. Purebred dogs and dogs of unknown pedigree. Dogs with collars and licenses, and dogs with none.

Inside, the room was surprisingly warm and cozy. The dogs took their places facing the front, where a small podium stood ready. The room was

filled with sound, excited yips and barks, but
became silent as an old dog moved toward the
podium. His hair was graying at the beard, and
his walk had lost the spring of youth, but his eyes
shone bright. In his mouth he held a manuscript.
He looked out at the group, carefully placed the
papers at his feet, and began to speak.

"Welcome, canine friends. Welcome to the
meeting of the WOOF Society—Words of Our

Friends. I, Beauregard, your president, am proud to
see such a large gathering for this groundbreaking
meeting. Let's repeat our motto. All together
now!"

The dogs began to chant their motto, each in a
different voice.

"WOOF! WOOF! WOOF!"

Beauregard closed his eyes in satisfaction, then
examined the crowd.

"As you can see, we have a packed house tonight, so if some of the Chihuahuas wouldn't mind sharing seats, then we'll get started. We all know why we're here, so I won't waste time. Oh, I see a paw raised in the second row. Yes, Pap, you have a question."

An old hound dog blinked. "Why are we here? I forgot. I'm fifteen years old, but remember, that's a hundred and five in people years."

"Yes, Pap, good question. I'll start at the beginning. As you know, for years we have been working to promote a worldwide understanding that dogs have vocabularies beyond *sit*, *stay*, and *fetch*, that we are indeed accomplished storytellers. Through the dedicated efforts of our membership,

4

we have been collecting stories from dogs across the world and throughout history. Tonight we will be hearing some of those stories."

"Mr. President?"

"Yes, a question from the Newfoundland in the back."

"Will there be any rescue stories?"

"Of course. Daring canine heroes have rescued countless masters from the perils of avalanche and fire. And courageous companions have accompanied their owners into battles and across continents in exploration. There will be a variety of stories, rescue and other-wise."

"What about history?" said a Basset Hound. "I love history."

"Yes, Professor Basset. All through the ages, dogs have faced challenges and had stories to tell. From ancient Egypt to Pompeii to the days of early America. . . . The poodle in the back."

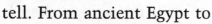

"Well, I hope it's not all history. Today we face new challenges, like bark collars, electric fences—and what about powder-resistant fleas?"

At the mention of fleas, fierce scratching broke out among the members. A small black puppy rolled on his back and wiggled.

"Order, friends," Beauregard said sternly. "We will cover some contemporary issues. Question from the Shih Tzu."

"I hope it's not going to be all stories from big dogs."

"No, there will be stories from many divisions of our canine kingdom, big and small, past and present, smart and . . . well . . . let's just say there will be something for everyone. Question from the small mixed-breed in the second row."

"Who goes first?"

"We will begin with a manuscript from Egypt. Jack's master is an archaeologist, and while his master was digging, Jack did some digging of his own. This was found near a stela from the Eleventh Dynasty. It tells the story of the reign of Intef.

But on the back, unnoticed by humans, is another story, the story of one of our ancestors named Abu, who was the ruler of Egypt."

Excited yips and howls broke out.

"Order! Order! Come to order. The presenters will come forward one at a time and read their stories."

The dogs leaned forward expectantly as a scholarly-looking Jack Russell Terrier came forward, carrying a small piece of butcher paper.

"Now, without further ado, the WOOF Society presents what we have come to call *Dog Diaries*."

CHAPTER 2

Abu: The Dog Who Ruled Egypt

Egypt, circa 2000 B.C.
Read by Jack

I am the ruler of Egypt.

This is how I know that I am the ruler of Egypt: When I bark, the royal cook rushes to fill up my bowl. He is my servant. When I stand by the door, the royal door opener opens the door for me. He too is my servant. When I stand beside my human, Intef, at the royal throne, people come and bow down. They all serve me! I must be the Pharaoh! All bow before Abu!

My human brushes my sleek hair. His son massages my back and rubs behind my ears. A-h-h! They call me Abu. They too are my servants.

I am great! I am powerful! I am totally in charge! All serve me! Except . . . there is only one who does not serve me. One who does not bow down and serve Abu. One who is disobedient to me. It is Miu, the Royal Cat.

When my human rides in the royal chariot, I lead the way, running fast and moving sleekly. I call out, "Look at me! Look at me! Make way for Abu!"

I lead them past the pyramids and past the giant Sphinx. I lead them into battle, fearless of the arrows and spears that fall around me. I hunt the giant ostrich and keep pace with him step by step. No man or beast can run faster than Abu. I keep pace with the mighty hart as we hunt. I keep pace with the hare. I am the fastest in the world! No beast can escape me. Except . . . there is only one who can escape me. Only one who can race away, jumping to heights that I cannot attain. It is Miu, the Royal Cat.

I have learned to always be in control, to sit with my human at the royal throne, head up and back straight. I have learned to lead the chariots, running straight as an arrow, not looking left or right. I have learned to wait by the door, standing calm and regal. Abu is always totally in control. Always calm and cool and still as the Sphinx. Nothing can make me lose my control. Except...

only one thing can make me lose my control. One creature who can turn me into a scrambling, drooling, running, barking fool. My hair rises unbidden on my back. My lips curl into an unkindly snarl. My front teeth bare. It is Miu, the Royal Cat.

No one touches Abu's royal food bowl. The servants prepare the best for me—roasted tender meat. No one comes near, my bowl is only for the royal Abu. Except one. My water is pure water carried from the royal well. No one touches my water. No one dares to defile the royal water bowl. Except one. And no one dares to sit on Abu's cushion under the throne. Except one—Miu. Miu! MIU, the Royal Cat!

At night I, Abu, sleep in the royal kennel. There are embroidered pillows and comfortable cushions just for my comfort. But . . . it is dark in the royal kennel and a little cold. Sometimes when I am in the kennel and it is cold and dark, I don't feel so much like the ruler of Egypt. I try to be brave. I call out, "I am the Pharoah! I am brave! I am not afraid." My human sleeps in the royal chambers in the palace, his son in the nursery.

The servants and guards have their own places. The royal kennel is a wonderful place, a worthy place for Abu. But . . .

Sometimes when I am lonely, I curl up and close my eyes and long for the morning to come. Sometimes when I am lonely at night, I sleep and hope to dream happy dreams. Sometimes I feel like there is no hope that morning will come. I am all alone. Except . . .

I feel something warm snuggle against my back, and I don't move. I listen to soft breathing and then a low purr. It is Miu, the Royal Cat. And with the comfort of the warmth on my back, I fall asleep.

CHAPTER 3

Einstein: What's in a Name?

I got a new name today, and it is the perfect name. What's in a name, you say? Not much, or so I thought. Now I know differently.

I was born Claudius Augustus III, and the family called me Gussy. I had a little wiggle in my walk, and I felt like a Gussy.

Then my family moved away, and I went to a place called the dog shelter.

The lady there did not call me Gussy. She called me Claudius. After a few days, I didn't walk with a wiggle anymore. I walked with dignity. When I ate, I ate carefully, not rushed and sloppy like the other dogs. I felt like a Claudius.

There were lots of dogs at the pound, and slowly I began to notice that the name matched the dog. The dog in the cage next to me was named Prissy, and that's what she was. Prissy did not like to get her feet wet, and when she did, she would spend thirty minutes licking them clean.

Sergeant was next. His cage was orderly—toys in one corner, bed in the other. If a worker accidentally put a toy in the wrong place, Sergeant would move it back to the correct corner.

On the other side of me was Sneaky, always hiding his toys and stealing extra food. Then there was Baby, constantly rolling over into a submissive position. On the end was T-Rex. I never went in the run with T-Rex!

After only a few days at the shelter, I knew my theory was correct. The name made the dog!

One day a family came to the shelter and took me home. My first night, they were talking about choosing a name for me. Knowing how important a name is, I listened carefully. My life depended on it.

I wondered what my new name might be. Would it be something grand, like King or Prince? Or something military like Captain or Major? I

hoped it didn't end in *O*, like Oleo, Waldo, Dumbo, Romeo . . . well, maybe all *O* names aren't so bad.

I wanted the perfect name.

"What about TJ?" the man said.

"What's that stand for?" the lady asked.

"Nothing. I just like initials."

"It has to stand for something."

"How about Cinderella?" the girl said.

I held my breath until someone said, "No."

"How about Spot?" the man said.

The lady looked me over. "He doesn't have any spots. It needs to be right."

Finally, someone was realizing the importance of this decision.

"I've got it," the man said. "The dog seems pretty smart. He can fetch and sit and roll over. Let's put him on the other side of the room and see what he responds to."

So, they put me by the chair. They sat on the sofa. Then, they called out names.

"Checkers. Domino. Uno."

No games, please.

"Utah. Dakota. Tex."

No states, please.

"Buckwheat. Muffin. T-Bone."

Could I hear the states again?

I did not move for any of those names.

"Wait! I just thought of the perfect name," the woman said.

My ears perked up. What was this perfect name?

"Einstein."

I wagged my tail. It sounded interesting.

"You mean Einstein the brilliant scientist?" the girl asked.

A brilliant scientist—I liked that even better.

"Perfect for a smart dog. Let's try it," the man said.

They looked at me, and together they called out, "Einstein."

I jumped up and ran to the family. I extended my paw in a handshake.

Einstein is the perfect name for me. I feel brilliant. In fact, I feel so brilliant I could sing, "I feel brilliant, oh so brilliant. . . ."

CHAPTER 4

Pooch's Invisible Enemy

I don't like the new house. There is another
animal here. It's under the sink. I can't see it, but
I can hear it.

It gets all the good food. I get dry stuff. It eats three times a day. I am lucky to eat once.

When it gets fed, I bark and bark. I'm saying, "I'll eat that moldy meat. I love moldy meat."

They say, "Quiet, Pooch," and "What's gotten into Pooch?"

I'm saying, "I love greenish cheese, burnt toast, stale pork rinds."

They say, "Quiet, Pooch."

Today I made some progress. I learned the name of the animal. It is called Disposal, and when I get my paws on Disposal, he is going down the drain!

CHAPTER 5

Dawg Strikes Gold

Colorado, 1892
Read by Professor Bassett

MORNING

We're on our way out of town. Sam on his horse, Hoss. Me trailing behind. I get tired of looking at Hoss's rear end, but Hoss don't like me. If he see me in front or to one side, he try to bite. You ever take a good look at a horse's teeth? You rather see his rear end.

Sam talking to Hoss. Why he waste his time like that? Hoss don't understand. Hoss barely understand "whoa." What's worse, Sam talking 'bout robbing a stagecoach. Hoss shaking his head back and forth like he don't want no part of that. Maybe Hoss understand more than I think he do.

Hoss don't want to get caught and strung up. Me neither.

NOON

The town we leaving be called Bad News. It live up to its name. We fit right in. We be low on money, low on food, low in spirit. And we head out with not much more than we brung in. Sam still talking about holding up the stagecoach. Hoss shaking his head.

Then stagecoach pass us, going fast, making dust. We lucky we still standing. Then Sam don't talk about stagecoaches no more.

NIGHT

We camp. Sam cook some beans with pork mixed in. When he get full, I get the rest. I lick the pan clean. That way I don't miss nothing, and nobody have to wash it.

I be thirsty, but I don't go to the creek right away. Hoss be there first. Hoss always be at the water first. He roll in it. He snort in it. If he feel like it, he pee in it. I wait awhile for the water to get clean.

I stop on the bank because Hoss slosh water up on the bank. I see funny little rocks lying on the mud. I pick one up, carry it to the fire, and drop it in the pan.

Sam say, "Dawg, don't be spitting in the eating dish. It ain't polite."

Then Sam take a look and he yelled, "Gold! You found gold!" Then he shut up because if some-body hear him, they be all over Cripple Creek.

MORNING

Hoss and me be back at Cripple Creek.
Hoss messing it up, splashing out
water. Me picking up gold.
Sam sitting on the bank.
He hold the pan. That
be his part of gold
mining.

NOON
More gold mining.

NIGHT
More gold mining.

MORNING

More gold mining. We be at Cripple Creek for a long, long time, doing this every day. When Sam get all the gold he can carry, which was all the gold there was in the creek, we head out. Sam on Hoss.

Hoss and me buddies by this time, side by side. I'm not looking at his rear no more. Everybody be happy. Our gold mining days be over.

CHAPTER 6

Tidbit: A Star Is Born

Nashville, Tennessee, 1957
Read by Beauregard

I was born the smallest of the litter. Even as a pup I had to fight to survive. While my brothers and sisters grew up to be fast and strong and to jump high, I grew up to be a beggar. While my brothers and sisters grew up handsome and sleek, I grew up ugly. I was a pitiful young thing, but even pitiful young things can have remarkable experiences in life—moments that change a life from pitiful to significant. This is one.

I took to the streets young, living beside Dumpsters or hanging out at the back doors of restaurants. I lived hand-to-mouth. I made the rounds in Nashville each morning, hoping the trash had been carelessly emptied behind the restaurants or that someone had not finished a Big Mac. I had no home. I lived a dangerous life, avoiding kicks and yells.

One day as I was making my usual rounds, I heard a noise coming from the back door of a building. It was a wonderful sound. A rhythmic *boom boom*. A soft gliding sound. A plunking and a twanging, all harmoniously rolled together. A sound that for the first time made me feel like I was home. I parked myself at that door, the back door to the Grand Ole Opry.

People coming in and out of the Opry are good people. They began to notice me, but instead of kicking and yelling at me, they were kind. They brought me snacks and patted my head.

I watched every night as a parade of boots went through that door. Lizard-skin boots, ostrich, elephant-skin—every color of the rainbow. There were amazing costumes in shiny patterns and tall, wide hats. They were fancy people, but they were kind. Someone gave me a blanket one day. Once, I got a whole pork chop.

Then one day I got something I thought I never would have in this world. A woman in a sequined dress with light blue boots bent down to give me a napkin full of small pieces of steak. But that wasn't all. She patted my head and said, "Here you go, Tidbit." *Tidbit!* I had a name. I had a home. I longed for a master, and above all I longed to go inside. I wondered, Would she take me inside? "Come on, Dolly," someone called. And she was gone.

I listened every day to the music. The *boom boom* was a bass. The gliding sound, a fiddle. The plunk, a banjo; the twang, a guitar. Best of all were the voices. When I listened to the voices, my tail would thump. Then my body would twitch, then my nose would begin to rise up, and if the music was just right and just wonderful enough: *AOOOOOOOO!* A sound worked up from the bottom of my belly to the back of my throat and let loose a long, mournful howl.

Alone behind the Opry, I learned to sing.

Sometimes the people would gather at the back door with their instruments. They would play together, working out a little piece of music to perfection, or just making the music for the joy of it. I sat quietly on my blanket and listened. A man named Charles made the fiddle sing. The banjo jumped in the hands of Scruggs. A man named Porter had the glitteriest coat of all.

One time a different man came. A man with the blackest boots and tallest hat that I had ever seen. A man with the lowest, smoothest voice that I

had ever heard. A man dressed all in black. He sang about trains and prisons and someone called Mama. He sang in the voice of pain and sorrow and too many nights out on the blanket. And my tail began to thump, my body to twitch, my nose to point up, up, and *AOOOOOOOO*. I joined his song.

"Hey, Johnny, you got some company," the fiddle player said. Everyone laughed, but the music went on. Johnny and I sang one song after another. Then the fiddle player looked at me and said the words that would change my life, "Let's take Tidbit on the Opry."

Everyone stopped and looked down at me. I waited until I could stand it no more, then *AOOOOOOOO*. That did it. They all laughed, and the man in black picked me up.

"Ten minutes!" someone called from the door, and in we went. I had never been inside. It was beautiful and warm. Then the fiddle player tied a red bandanna around my neck, and we walked onto the stage. I sat beside the black boots and looked out.

I had never seen so many people before. Cameras flashed, people clapped. I got so nervous I almost wet the stage, but I stood tight and— *boom boom*—the bass began. The gliding fiddle

joined in. Plunk and twang, and Johnny was singing about Mama.

I listened at first, too stunned to do anything. And then I was swept away by the sounds. My tail did not move at first, but as he sang on, my tail started thumping, my body started twitching, and my nose rose.

AOOOOOOOO.

I no longer saw the crowds or the cameras.

I was lost in the music, singing with Johnny.

I was home.

When the music ended, there was quiet at first, then it all broke loose. I looked out and saw the people. They were cheering and clapping and jumping up and down. For that moment and forever after, my life was different.

If you saw me now, you might think that my life hadn't changed much. I'm still pretty sad to look at, but I am not so hopeless after all. I wear my bandanna and ride in the bus with Johnny, right up in the front seat. Every once in a while, when it's a slow night on stage, Johnny picks me up and says, "Sing one, Tidbit," and my tail begins to thump, then my body begins to twitch, and I lift up my nose and join right in, *AOOOOOOOO!*

CHAPTER 7

Marcus: A Mountain Comes Alive

Italy, A.D. 79
Read by Jack

For several days I knew something was wrong. The ground would tremble slightly, sometimes leaving small cracks in the wall. Occasionally I would get a whiff of a strange scent.

Then, on August 24, life changed forever. I was sound asleep in the garden when I was awakened by an earsplitting *boom*. A second *boom* quickly followed. Suddenly, the people in my household were in the garden with me. They were looking up at the mountain they call Vesuvius. A large, dark cloud hung over Vesuvius, and it appeared to be moving slightly toward our city, Pompeii.

Then, a light gray ash began to fall from the sky.

"The mountain is alive," screamed one of the slaves.

My master called for us to go to one of the lower rooms of the house. I followed, although it is not what I wanted to do. Everyone entered the room. I stood at the door. The children, huddled in one corner, called to me.

"Come, Marcus. Come."

I would not enter the room.

"Come, Marcus," my mistress called. I stood fast.

The ground trembled again, and my master reached for me. The second before he grabbed my collar, I darted away. I bolted up the stairs, through the corridor to the front door.

Outside, men, women, and children ran in all directions. Some fled toward the sea, others toward the city gates. Yet others seemed to be running nowhere at all, calling the names of loved ones. Ash continued to fall, leaving a gray, powdery dust on everything. It made the people look like moving statues.

Those running to the sea probably hoped to escape by boat. I decided to go to the countryside. I would exit through the gates. Not the Vesuvius Gate—that would lead directly to the trouble. I would use the Sarno Gate by the amphitheater and run as fast as I could for as long as I could.

I ran along the city streets, darting between legs. The cloud caused darkness all around, which made it difficult to see. Some people carried torches, hoping to light the way, but it was useless. Small stones fell from the sky, knocking out the torches.

I kept running—past people carrying their possessions, past people carrying children, past slaves carrying their owners' wealth. People fell all around me. Bodies littered the streets. Ash rained down onto my head, and fiery stones burst into flames at my feet. My eyes burned from the ash.

I passed shops. People huddled in the doorways for shelter. I did not stop. If I stopped for even a moment, death would be on me like flies on meat in the butcher shop.

Ash covered the street and my paws. I could tell

there would come a point when it would be so deep that I would no longer be able to run. So I ran faster, jumping over obstacles, darting between legs.

Finally I reached the Sarno Gate. All I could see was legs—moving but going nowhere. People were screaming. I tried to push my way through but did not get far. I tried a different direction. A person collapsed in front of me.

If I did not get out the gate I would die! I pushed past one leg, then another. It's a good thing I'm a skinny dog. I continued to weave between legs.

For a while, it seemed like I was making no progress at all. Then, finally, I broke free into the countryside.

I turned for another look at Vesuvius. It was more frightening than before. The smoke from the top looked like a great tree with branches on all sides. The cloud extended from the mountain all the way down.

As I watched, one large section on top of the mountain swayed slightly. It swayed again. Then, with a tremendous crashing sound, it gave way and collapsed down the side of the mountain. Following behind it was a gush of fire and burning melted rock, all rolling toward Pompeii.

The earth shook. I fell. People around me fell too. Some did not get up.

I ran and never looked back. I did not know when day ended and night began, I kept running. Finally, I came to some large rocks. I crawled between the rocks and sank into a deep sleep.

When I awoke, I discovered a young boy had crawled in beside me. I curled up next to the boy. We stayed side by side until daylight returned two days later.

I never did find my family. I tried once to get back into Pompeii, but the ground was too hot. Now, I live with the boy and his family on a farm on the hillside. Vesuvius is still there, but it looks caved in and ragged. When I see it, I think about August 24—the day the mountain came alive.

CHAPTER 8

Roscoe: Love Is in the Air

For weeks I have been trying to impress the Poodle next door. Her name is Venus. She was named for the Roman goddess of love and beauty. And, boy, is she beautiful! Soft white hair, easy curls, dark mysterious eyes, and a smell that will make you drool. Any dog would be glad just to stand beside her. My goal in life is to win Venus.

The only thing holding me back is Tiger, the cat who lives at my house. Tiger is big, fast, and the best hunter I've ever seen, bar none. She always seems to foil my plans.

This morning Tiger caught a squirrel. I have

been trying to catch squirrels for years, but just barely miss them every time. It's Tiger's fault. She gets them first.

Tiger's squirrel was an especially big one, and she left it in the front yard. So I'm thinking, "Now's my chance to show off." Venus was in her back yard. Perfect.

I get the squirrel and head her way. It feels good to have that squirrel in my mouth. I shake it a few times. Yes, it feels real good. Empowering.

Venus sees me. I hold that squirrel up high where she can see it. She is looking at me like I am some fine Labrador. This makes me feel great, so I toss that squirrel around. I toss once. I toss twice. I toss . . .

Then I see Tiger come around the corner. She sniffs the spot where her squirrel was. She sniffs some more. Then she sees me. The squirrel is still in my mouth, but I no longer feel empowered.

I know what you're thinking: You're a brave dog. You don't have anything to worry about. Finders keepers, losers weepers, and all that. Well, you don't know Tiger. She is a monster. She could bring a full-grown Saint Bernard to his knees.

I look at Venus. She is watching Tiger.

Tiger charges across the yard, stops in front of me, and hisses. I drop the squirrel. This is the right thing to do because otherwise she will scratch me in the face, and that would be a worse embarrassment.

Tiger takes her squirrel. Venus goes back into her house. I pee on the spot where I dropped the squirrel and go back into my house. Tomorrow is another day.

45

CHAPTER 9

Mimi's Guide to Life

Paris, France

BATHROOM PROTOCOL

People prefer to send you outside to do your business. This is fine and pleases them. This is fine, that is, if the weather permits.

In sunny weather, a bush or a patch of soft grass is perfectly acceptable.

In rainy or snowy or otherwise disagreeable weather, feel free to use the carpet or floor, but be sure to hide it. Behind a chair is a good spot. Closets work. Anywhere dark and out of the way.

I know a Basset Hound who got through an entire winter going in the guestroom under a double bed.

HIDING

Another of life's important skills for the canine is *hiding*. Hiding is necessary when normal dog activities are not acceptable to people. These might include improper snitching from the table, nipping and growling, and bathroom indiscretion. Hide under large objects—beds and sofas are ideal. Smaller furniture, chairs, and tea tables may work for Toy Poodles and Cocker Spaniels.

Position yourself where people can't reach. The center underneath a king-size bed is perfect. Watch out for the groping hand that will try to catch you. If you hide long enough, you will be forgiven. I once knew a Boxer who hid under a porch for three days following an unfortunate incident with a birthday cake.

TABLE MANNERS

Sit quietly and calmly beside the table. Above all, don't let your eagerness show. Jumping up, drooling, or loud moans of hunger can result in being "put out." Pay attention. Is there one particularly messy eater? (Babies fit into this category.) If so, align yourself beside this person and wait for fallout. If someone looks at you with a smile, go directly to that person and assume the position— sitting up on hind legs. The longer you can balance on your hind legs, the bigger the payoff.

CHAPTER 10

Bo versus Bank Robber

Bus stop.

I love school lunches!

I find them after the school bus leaves. They're in brown paper bags left on the sidewalk. My favorite school lunch is a bologna sandwich and a Twinkie.

Today I was on my way home from the bus stop, and I cut through a back yard. A man was getting out of the car. He put something on the ground and leaned back into the car to talk on one of those things people talk on.

I saw what he had put on the ground—a large

school lunch! There was writing on the bag, but I can't read people writing.

I grabbed it and took off. He yelled and took off after me.

I know neighborhood shortcuts, so I went through hedges, and he had to go around. I got home and went in my dog door. A person I live with named Sissy was getting ready to cook something.

She stopped me and said, "Bad dog. What have you got now? Give me that."

I had worked hard for this school lunch, and I wasn't about to give it up. But she pressed a certain spot on my neck and my mouth opened. It didn't want to open, but it had to. I hate when they do this. Half the time they do it and then put something round in your mouth and make you swallow it. Your throat does not want to swallow it, but it has to.

She opened the bag and yelled, "Mom!" Mom is another person I live with.

I HAVE A GUN PUT THE MONEY IN THE BAG!

Sissy and Mom met in the hall, and Sissy showed her the bag. I wanted to say, "Hey! It's my school lunch."

Mom read the bag aloud, "I have a gun. Put the money in the bag."

Apparently the bag was full of money, a lot of it, and Sissy wanted them to split it, and Mom said that wouldn't be right. And Sissy said something else, and Mom said something about robbers or drug dealers, and then there was a knock on the back door. A voice said, "I want my bag." Usually I run to the back door and bark when somebody knocks, but this time I didn't.

Sissy and Mom looked at each other, dropped the bag, and ran into a bedroom and locked the door.

What about me?

I grabbed the bag, went into the other bedroom, and hid under the bed. Because, sure, there was money in the bag, but that didn't mean there wasn't a bologna sandwich along with it.

There was a terrible noise. The man was beating on the back door and shaking the door and finally kicking down the door and coming in the house. Usually I would be doing what they call "barking my head off" at this, but I didn't.

The man came down the hall and kicked in the bedroom door. I heard Sissy and Mom scream and then there was some talk and Sissy called, "Bo, come here, Bo," in a voice that was higher than usual. I didn't come.

Then mom sang out, "Bo! Bo! Din-ner!"

And I came.

Sometimes I act like I don't have any sense at all. I ran into the kitchen to my bowl, but it was empty. A trick. I still had the bag in my mouth, so I went out my dog door and kept running.

I paused at the hedge and saw the man come out, followed by Sissy and Mom. The man had a gun in his hand. I've seen those on TV. And he pointed it at me! At me!

Sissy cried, "Oh, no, don't you shoot my Bo." And she hit him with a weapon of her own—the frying pan. She had managed to hold on to that throughout everything.

The man fell down, and at that moment, two men in uniform came around the house. It was the police. Mom had called them while she and Sissy were hiding in the bedroom.

The police took the man and the money. And Sissy and Mom and I went back into the house. I got my picture in the newspaper—there's something about a dog catching a bank robber that people enjoy. I also got a T-bone steak.

A T-bone steak is something you never get in a school lunch, so everything worked out fine.

CHAPTER 11

Jip: The Long Way Home

Virginia, 1864
Read by Professor Bassett

THIS WAS THE DAY WE LEFT OAK FALLS. Me and Jim Jr. were going to war. I didn't know exactly what war was, but I knew it was something serious and that Jim Jr. might need me.

We were in the yard, ready to leave. Jim Jr.'s mother hugged him so tight that she felt my body, which was inside his coat. She drew back.

"Junior! You aren't taking Jip with you," she said.

"Jip wants to go, don't you, boy?" He opened the top of his coat, and I looked out. Deep inside the coat my tail wagged in agreement. Jim Jr. said, "We'll take care of each other, Mama."

"See that you do," she said. She pointed her finger at me. "You're too young to go to war." Then she pointed at her son. "And so are you."

"Mama, I'm almost eighteen."

They hugged again. Big Jim hugged him too and said, "Farewell, son."

Now that I'd been discovered, there was no point in hiding in the coat, so he set me on the ground and we started up the road.

At the bend in the road, Jim Jr. looked back at the farm. It was like he had to take the farm away with him, like it was the last time he'd ever see it.

"Farewell," he said quietly, and we continued on our way.

THIS WAS THE DAY AFTER THE BATTLE. Now I knew what war was. It was terrible noises and smells and cries of pain and pleas for help. I stayed with Jim the best I could. Late in the day he fell down hard, and I hid under his coat until it was over. His hand lay on my head. From time to time, he would moan and his hand would wander, but I found it every time and wiggled under it.

When dawn broke, he said, "Jip?" in a weak way. Then, louder, "Jip!" I crawled out and lay my head on his shoulder. "Is it night?" he asked.

He didn't say anything more. After a bit, two men came, looked him over, and picked him up, one at his shoulders, one at his legs. I followed them to a tent. They stopped me from going inside. I don't know how long this went on.

THIS WAS THE DAY WE STARTED HOME. Jim still couldn't see, but a man who'd made harnesses and such before the war rigged up a sort of harness for me. Ropes went around my chest in a certain way, and Jim held on to the whole thing. Jim said if they could get him on a train to Oak Junction, we could walk the rest of the way.

On the train ride I sat on Jim's lap, and people fed us things. When the train got to Oak Junction, I didn't want to get off.

Jim knew how to start off to Oak Falls, but he got tired quick. When he started stumbling, I found us shelter in a barn. We were the only animals there.

In the morning, the farmer came out and his wife gave us breakfast. He said the army had taken his horses, or he would've driven us home. Jim thanked him for breakfast, and we set off.

It was hard going. I did my best, but I would walk under a tree, and a low limb would knock him down. Or I wouldn't see a rock and he'd trip. Every time he said, "Keep going, Jip. You're doing fine."

We spent another night under a bridge to keep out of the rain, but we didn't mind because Jim and I both remembered the bridge. It wasn't far from home. During the night, he kept saying, "Is it morning, Jip?" because he wanted to get going. Finally, it was morning and we set out.

We were wet, but I just shook the water off and Jim didn't seem to care. We turned down our road, and I didn't have to lead him anymore. He knew this road. When we went around the bend, he stopped.

I looked up at him, and his face was turned to the farm. He was all smiles. He said, "Jip, I never thought I'd see this place again."

He gave a whoop, and the family burst out the door and ran to meet us.

CHAPTER 12

Lucy's Blended Family

Dear Diary,

It's been weeks since I've written you, and as you read this you will see why.

Seven weeks ago, on a cold January day, I delivered three puppies. My owner was there, and together we admired my beautiful puppies.

One morning several weeks later, I was nursing my pups when the phone rang. It was obvious something was wrong—a crisis. My owner kept looking at me and saying my name. The crisis concerned me.

She hung up the phone, turned to me, and said two of my favorite words, *car ride.*

I didn't usually leave the puppies, but I do love a car ride. She closed the puppies up in the laundry room, and we headed for the car.

Ten minutes later, we pulled into the vet's parking lot. THE VET. I hate that place. I jumped in the back seat. My owner opened the back door. I jumped in the front seat. Finally, she picked me up and we went inside. Immediately I realized that this was not a typical visit. The lady in the front quickly led us to a back room where I'd never been before.

The first thing I noticed was a big box on the floor. What was in the box? Why were we there? What was that high squeaking noise?

My owner lifted me up, and I looked into the box. Two small kittens huddled in the corner. Then, without warning, she lowered me into the box. I trusted her, but this was strange.

I stood there in the box, with the two small kittens just inches away. They looked weak and tired, and I didn't know what was expected of me.

"Lie down, Lucy," my owner said.

I lay down.

The lady picked up one of the kittens and placed it right next to one of my nipples. I looked at the lady, then at my owner. They were holding their breath.

The kitten sniffed my nipple, then licked it. Suddenly, she grabbed my nipple and began to nurse. The second kitten grabbed another nipple. He started to nurse too. They nursed hard. I wondered when they'd had their last meal and where their mother was. Then it struck me. Now I was their mother.

I looked up to see smiles on the faces of my owner and the lady. Clearly, they were pleased that these kittens were getting something to eat. I was pleased too. I leaned back and relaxed.

Next thing I knew, they were loading the box, with me and the kittens, into the car.

The kittens are at our house now, and my puppies love them.

I never expected to have a blended family, but I wouldn't change a thing.

CHAPTER 13

WOOF! WOOF! Till Next Year

All was chaos! Some dogs were howling, other pounding their paws to the floor in thunderous applause. Tails wagged and bodies wiggled in delight. Beauregard made his way slowly back to the podium. He choked back tears.

"Never," he said, "never before have we heard such a thing as this . . . *Dog Diaries*. These stories prove that dogs do have vital stories to tell. You, my friends, have been a part of dog history. This concludes the first annual meeting of the WOOF Society."

The noise and wiggling and howling and thumping broke out again.

"Order," said the president. "Order! I have one more very important announcement before the night is over."

The crowd quieted.

"Are there refreshments?" a drooling Peke in the third row asked hopefully.

"No food. Something more important. At our next meeting we will be joined by the cat society, MEOW (Memories Expressed in Our Writing)."

A Doberman in the front row raised his back hair and growled. Beauregard gave him the harsh stare of the Alpha dog. "Remember, Canine Friends," he said not taking his eyes off the offender, "we value *all* writers, and the members of MEOW must be treated with dignity and respect." The Doberman's tail drooped.

Beauregard continued, "Perhaps this would be a good time for Calvin to read some of his New Year's Resolutions. Calvin."

Calvin made his way to the podium.

"My list is not complete, but here's what I've got so far.

"One. I will not bark when the phone rings.

"Two. I will not bunch up the covers on the bed.

"Three. I will not chase cats when I am on a leash.

"Four. I will not chase cats if there is any possibility I might catch them.

Of course, now that I know they are fellow authors, I wouldn't chase them at all . . . if I could help it," he said with a wink to the audience.

"Five. I will not hug ladies' legs.

"Six. I will not smell people's personal places.

"I know these are the same resolutions I made last year . . .

and the year before. So, here is my most important resolution—I will keep my New Year's Resolutions."

The crowd cheered as Calvin sat down.

"Until next time," Beauregard said, "hold high our motto, and remember to share it with your human friends. All together now!"

"WOOF! WOOF! WOOF!"

From the abandoned building, under the rickety stairwell, one by one the dogs emerged. Large Dobermans, small Pekingese, Scotties, and Pugs. Purebred dogs and dogs of unknown pedigree.

Dogs with collars and licenses, and dogs with none.

They were all different, but all had three things in common: They were dogs. They were literate. And most important their tails were wagging.

You've heard from Abu, the dog who ruled Egypt—now meet Miu, Abu's feline rival. Hear how Chico, the world's smallest cat, stops a crime. The Pirate Cat doesn't just find mice, she finds treasure, too.

It turns out dogs aren't the only ones with a secret society. . . .

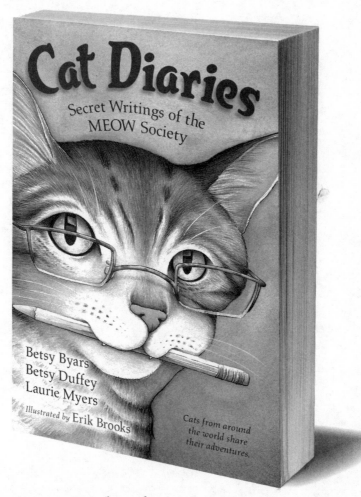

Read on for an excerpt.

CHAPTER 1

Full Moon, Empty Streets

It was the third full moon of the year when cats around the world began to disappear. The alleys and streets were quiet. Trash cans stood untouched, lids strangely in place. Dogs sniffed the air anxiously while mice ran freely, unafraid of predators. Music drifted from apartment windows, unaccompanied by feline howls.

The cat population had a meeting to attend. Large and small, old and young, cats headed to an old abandoned theater. When the room was filled, the eyes of the cats focused toward the front, where

a large gray cat with battle scars made his way to the
stage. He spoke.

"I, Ebenezer, call the meeting to order."

"This better be good," called a calico from the back. "I had to plot for three days to get out of the house to come." A Siamese slunk back and forth along the sideline. "And I don't have claws, so I took a big risk getting here."

A fat cat yelled, "It rained yesterday. You know how I hate to get my feet wet, but I did it just to get here, even though I heard we might be meeting with dogs."

"Dogs?" a kitten asked, shaking.

"That was just a rumor," Ebenezer said. "There was some discussion about a possible meeting with the WOOF Society, Words of Our Friends. You see, dogs have written diaries too."

"Dogs? Diaries? Our dog can't even clean himself," a cat yelled.

"How many dogs have enough sense to write a diary?" said an alley cat.

"I agree. The dog in my house could no more write a diary than climb a tree."

"Not so fast," Ebenezer said. "I've read some dog diaries. The stories are not bad."

Yowls erupted. Ebenezer waited for the sounds to die down, then spoke. "On to our business."

"Tell us more," called a young cat from the third row. "This is my first meeting."

"As many of you know, for some time now we have been collecting writings by members of our feline community. We call this group MEOW (Memories Expressed in Our Writing)."

Meows of agreement echoed throughout the room. A paw went up.

"Yes, Cisco."

Cisco cleared his throat.

"Hairball," someone yelled from the back. Several cats laughed. Others coughed.

"Order!" called Ebenezer. "Cisco, go ahead."

"What kinds of writings will we hear tonight?"

"There are many different tales."

"Not from the Manx," someone yelled. "They don't have tails."

Everyone laughed, except the Manxes, who hissed.

Ebenezer continued. "Throughout history, cats in their own quiet way have been writing stories—stories of their lives and the lives of others. Tonight, we will hear diaries from a Gypsy cat, a pirate cat, and many more."

"Let's get started," called an Abyssinian.

"We will begin with the diary of a cat named Fuzzy, who learned that it's a delicate balance to keep the best of both worlds. Now, get comfortable."

Some cats curled into balls, others tucked their front paws neatly underneath their bodies. Everyone settled into position and awaited the first reading.

"Fuzzy, please come forward for the reading of the first of the cat diaries."

❖ CHAPTER 2 ❖

Fuzzy's Two Worlds

DECEMBER 15

Today my family brought a tree into the house. You heard right, they brought a real tree *in*. This is a special treat for me because I don't go out much. Some cats love *out*. I don't. I love *in*, where it's warm.

When the tree first arrived I sniffed it over and over. I sat underneath the tree while my family hung things on it—fuzzy things, shiny things, round things, things of different shapes and sizes. My favorite is a shiny red ball. It's better than all my cat toys put together.

I plan to sleep under the tree all night and let the rich smell of pine fill my nostrils. Now that I have my own tree, my life is complete. I have the best of both worlds, *in* and *out*.

DECEMBER 16

Today my life is *not* complete. Today I do *not* have the best of both worlds.

This morning I was under the tree letting the smell of pine wash over me, when suddenly I had the most fantastic idea. I decided to *climb* the tree. I have sharp claws. I could do it.

I looked up. My red shiny ball was hanging on one of the top branches, swinging slightly as if to say, "Come on up."

"I'll be right there." I purred.

I tested the tree, first with one paw, then the other. It felt firm, solid. I started up, squeezing past branches, dodging lights. I was halfway up when I stopped to swat at a few items hanging from the outer branches. It was fun!

I continued to climb—past balls, past beads. Then I felt a slight sway. I stopped. It must have been my imagination. I moved slowly to the next branch. Another sway. I paused to give the tree a chance to settle down.

I gazed across the room. The view was fantastic. I could see everything. What a great spot! If I could get a little higher, it would be even better. I could stay there all day, and no one would be able to see me.

I moved carefully to the next branch. Yes indeed, this was perfect.

Wait a minute! Did the tree move again? No. Wait. Yes. It did move. It's moving more. This is not good. Not good at all. I think I'm going dooooooooown.

The tree crashed into the middle of the room, taking me with it. We hit the floor with balls and beads flying everywhere. Then it was quiet. I got up and shook myself off. What do you know? The shiny red ball was right at my feet. I batted it around a few times.

"Fuzzy?" someone yelled from another room.

"Fuzzy!" others cried, hurrying in.

I was beginning to get a bad feeling about this. They weren't happy. Someone picked me up.

"Fuzzy. OUT," someone yelled.

"*Out?*" I meowed. "I love *in*. Wait. Don't put me OOOOOOOOOOOOOOOOOOUT."

Slam. The door closed. Quickly I ran to the side window. Sometimes they let me *in* when I'm at that window.

"Here I am," I cried, shivering.

They ignored me.

"Let me IIIIIIIIIIN," I yelled.

They ignored me. They were busy fixing the tree.

"You know you're going to let me in eventually," I whimpered.

Then I noticed they were hanging my red shiny ball back on the tree, on that same high branch where the good view is. Suddenly, I was not worried.

I'm sure they will let me *in*, because they always do. Soon I will be warm. I will be back under my tree smelling the pine. I will climb to that high branch and sit next to my red shiny ball. Once again I will have the best of both worlds, *in* and *out*.

❧ CHAPTER 3 ❧

Rama, the Gypsy Cat

Kansas, 1900
Read by Ebenezer

DAY ONE

"Tonight the music is sad," the Gypsy woman said. I was on her lap, purring.

I have two purrs. Purr-one is a public purr. If anybody does something nice for me, I purr-one.

Purr-two is a private purr. It is deeper, warmer, for one person only. My purr-two is only for the Gypsy woman.

The Gypsy woman hummed and stroked my ears, my golden earring. She put the earring there when I was a kitten. She said, "Now you are a Gypsy like me. We Gypsies keep our eyes to the road ahead."

The Gypsy woman lifted my paw and looked at it. "I'll tell your future, Rama. What will tomorrow bring?"

She didn't like what she saw, for she dropped my paw and sighed.

A sudden breeze brought an interesting smell from the forest. I jumped to the ground.

"No, Rama, no!" she called after me. "Not tonight, Rama! Tonight we—" I never heard the rest.

I caught a mouse first thing, then a fat chipmunk. I saved the chipmunk's foot, a gift for the Gypsy woman.

Rain began to fall. I took shelter in a hollow tree. I was full. I was dry. I slept.

DAY TWO

The rain was harder, slanting into the hollow. I moved deeper inside.

By night I was hungry, but it was still raining. I wanted to be in the Gypsy woman's wagon. I wanted to be on her lap. I wanted to purr-two. I ate the chipmunk foot.

DAY THREE

I left the tree and ran to camp. The clearing was empty. The wagons were gone. The Gypsy woman was gone too.

I saw the wagon tracks and started to follow. I ran like the wind. I was hungry, but I didn't stop to hunt. I was thirsty, but I didn't stop to drink.

The wagon tracks stopped at the river. It was not a deep river. Horses and wagons could cross. Cats could not.

I continued to run, hoping to find a way across. At sundown I smelled smoke. Food was cooking.

I thought it was the Gypsy woman. Maybe she had not crossed the river with the others. She was waiting for me!

I ran to the clearing. I stopped. There was one wagon. It was not the Gypsy woman. A man sat by the wagon. He was singing, but it was not a Gypsy song.

"Too-rah-lie-ooooooh," he sang. The song ended. There was a silence.

I sat in the shelter of the trees and watched.